LaVon

alien

ANCESTORS

Kaya

Harbour

METATRON PRESS
WWW.METATRON.PRESS

the half-drowned
© 2022 Trynne Delaney

Published by Metatron Press
Montréal, Québec

First printing
Printed in Québec, Canada

All rights reserved

Editor | Shazia Hafiz Ramji
Cover art | Sidney Masuga
Copy editor | Kaiya Cade Smith Blackburn

Library and Archives Canada Cataloguing in Publication

Title: The half-drowned / Trynne Delaney.
Names: Delaney, Trynne, author.
Identifiers: Canadiana (print) 20220196680 | Canadiana (ebook) 20220196699 |
ISBN 9781988355252 (softcover) | ISBN 9781988355337 (PDF)
Classification: LCC PS8607.E48255 H35 2022 | DDC C813/.6—dc23

We acknowledge the support of the Canada Council for the Arts.

Canada Council   Conseil des arts
for the Arts   du Canada

THE HALF-DROWNED
TRYNNE DELANEY

METATRON PRESS
WWW.METATRON.PRESS

THE HALF-DROWNED

ANCESTORS: PROLOGUE	9
SWIMMING LESSONS	12
NIGHT ON MUD	16
'MEMBRINGS	26
PROPHET	28
HOW HE USED TO BE	32
NEW TOOTH	35
ALIEN FALLING	39
VENUS AT THE BATHS	41
WALK HOME	46
TRANSMISSIONS	52
CROSSROADS	56
GOLD DESIRES	58
CREATION MYTHS	67
SONGLESS	69
ANGELS	74
RITES	77
PAST FUTURE	83
SEEKING	88
HISTORY	94
RETURN	96
MELDING	99
ALIEN	101
ARRIVAL	102
IT MIRRORS I	106
RETURN II	110
AFTER MELDING	113
HOME	120
DEATH	124
END	126

TO SIMONE. YOU KNOW.

ANCESTORS: PROLOGUE

This is not a history lesson. You tucked in good? Then, let us tell you:

Backintheday, we worried about rogue waves, street checks, library fees, clean water, developers, all our cousins moving west for opportunity. On some calm weekend maybe our grandparents would take us out on the beach and we'd pretend there was no danger despite the omens: seal carcasses and plastic vomited onto shore. We turned away, threw bottle caps back out into the water, nested waste in more plastic bags.

All this destruction and we were only casual believers in endings.

Those rocks we used to climb crumbled tired sediments. Everything wasted down.

We used to live in old saltboxes, on farms, public housing, bungalows, apartments. Imagine the walls in a toxic salmon pink our parents chose to favour. Triangulated destiny: our homes placed us between a pulp mill, oil refinery, and nuclear power plant.

Big business employed us, let us rise in ranks when convenient.

Maybe ends didn't faze us 'cause they happened all the time.

But of course, you know our end came first with official papers scrawled in an unknown script, some hundreds of years ago—these small wounds of loss ulcerated within that large-mouthed hole. We became stolen people on stolen land. And so we stayed when everyone who could left for the sky. Before and after and always, here, our thousands of joys proliferated. We couldn't leave. Finally, we had the invitation to live on this land, in peace and friendship like we never did before on this purgatorial plane. We keep it simple: live as well as we can.

In the first floods there was euphoria even after we lost our homes. We had to move uphill into some unsteady yet permanent state of being earthbound. Sometimes we still buzz with the excitement of living through intentional destruction when we get a storm bad enough to make you sore but not enough to make you ache for generations. Everyone out in their wading pants finding something unexpected in the water. Looking down to where the silt has settled, a clear current runs, something sparkles from a crack in soggy pavement. Maybe it's fool's gold. Then again, sometimes what you thought you lost resurfaces.

And in these glittering moments, sometimes we choose to see good omens—the planet returning to some future whole.

SWIMMING LESSONS

Blue feet crumble off a cliff—I jump.

Backintheday, at the first migration, water was death.
Here, in the future, at last, I am learning to breathe underwater. I drown

Beneath the rippled crust is murky remembrance.
It's two years ago and I'm drowning because I want to. Recurrence is numbness. I drown
easily, chronically, in this atlantic, my mind, in what collects here in decay. I sink so deep my ribs rub up against a half-forgotten past
inaudible, out here surrounded by family. Peace. No death rattle. No scent but water. No taste but saline blood. No sight without stinging. I abandon lightness, sink

Underwater there's no bedrest, rot, scratching pus dried on sheets.
No panic, delirium, calamity, calmness.
Above, my eardrums beat in competition with rattling chests as they succumb to the thick rotting skin of embodiment.
baby playing with shells : death rattle

kettle before boil : death rattle
no one home : death rattles around, I drown,
they drown, up there, in their own bodies. I won't let myself. I will drown in some body elsewhere, here, again, two years ago.

Rolling around my skull, some echo of my own future, past luck, desires. Deep
fear deep fear deepening into hope buoys me, I break through the crust, I am steam erupted back to air, and presence.
I learned to swim to tempt fate with intention

All my friends are dead and so am I, even if I haven't left yet. This body belongs to something other than life. It reanimates for a few hours a day to make it home to Harbour, then returns to the bigger body of water. This body, a dead man, zombie, bones stretched against the knives of my bones. Skin pocked with rash from the toxic depths. I won't bathe. I'm not trying to be more clean and smooth. You think I should try to be more clean and smooth, that it will ease our bodies into some future wholeliness. You think it will ease the process. For you that's what swimming is like: clean and smooth, but that's not

what swimming feels like:
a rush,

washed back to shore and the rattle of rocks resisting the tide's pull.

Still, I am human.

Two years ago, when I was drowning, I became a beached whale. The water brought me back. Forced evolution. My fins became hands. I could no longer sing words in the right order. Speech on air was a death rattle.

shoes sifting through rocks to my body : death rattle
dry skin on salted skin : death rattle
dying engine of a search boat : death rattle, I was drowning, I'm

coated in plastics and I think I see my sister splayed, a lit beacon on the beach guiding me back to harbour. Her name: *Harbour*. Her purpose: *Harbour*. All I have to do is listen, watch my sister there, fetal, sleeping like the fishes, her mouth beckoning to air, her eyes beckoning to sight. Breathe air back into her quietly. Easy rescue. Easy harbouring of our souls side by side. Is this your gift to me? Some other prophecy you misread?

You murmur in my ear, you plead for me to stay, to let you hold me closer. I am not ready. You still think we might become one. I'm thinking of us as more zero sum.

Enough. I commit to the hug of shore. Cradle my sister's head in my rotten palms, stare down her mouth at the gift you've placed just past her wisdom, in the canyon of her gums. This gift, an ultimatum. You will take her if you cannot take me. Without knowing why, she will be forced to carry your desires. I can't manage resentment for you who knows no wrong.

I carry my Harbour home, up the hill, as your presence recedes with the water. It's not yet our time. When she wakes, I will return to you.

NIGHT ON MUD

On the new moon, after deep night falls and the orange fog of pollution settles, Harbour climbs over sandstone and bladderwrack onto the mud. It's dark out, dark as closed eyes under murky water. She wayfinds by the echo of a nearby cave, the light rush of a freshwater stream, the rotting meat of a washed up fish carcass. The shallowing crush of plastics beneath her feet tells her she's close to water.

Just two short generations ago, the expanse beyond the metres-high dunes of trash was a beach; now it's mud. It's said that bones—heavy enough to sink through the plastics—form the foundation of the mountains of detritus. It's also said that anyone foolish enough to venture out past the plastic walls that define shore from sea should be treated as a ghost until proven otherwise. Harbour keeps this and every other nightmare in mind as she wades out of the dunes and onto the rocks that soon dissolve to thick mud.

Her feet resist slippage. She's been here before, prays that will give her an advantage, though the landscape's shifted and crumbled into a different place than two years ago, two months ago even, two days.

Even before the last migration remade this place promised land, the mud would've been clear of people on impossible dark nights like this. Tide rises too fast here to take such risks. Before the last migration, no one needed to scavenge for resources or Rites. Back then, Rites consisted of:

> getting a car on a sixteenth birthday
> fucking the kid next door
> traveling to other continents
> living alone for the first time

No more. Rites beckon to a futurity that is as whole as it is absent as it is the past as it is unknowable. Or something. What everyone says is you can't know Rites 'til you do 'em. Maybe misguided, Harbour just wants to know what LaVon saw when he did his.

That past: the old folks all miss it sometimes, even if they won't say it because they fear people will talk. People do talk. They talk when they think the younger generations aren't listening. Tell tales about when you could go to Costco or Walmart and get anything you needed on shelves that reached the ceiling. Crouched beneath the community centre windows on the old folks' gathering days. Harbour has heard them calling out "God*damn* wouldn't this be easy with a Walmart instead of our makeshift marketplace." or "Don't you remember Costco hotdogs?" Longing. Harbour thinks she likes makeshift marketplaces better. Those old places were wasteful. At least, that's what the old folks had always taught. And yet, they still missed the excess. Everyone misses easy answers when the power shuts out for the night and they're left with only cooking oil firelight to counter shadow. In firelight everyone in town gets nostalgic for better and worse times, even if, like Harbour, this is the only time they know.

The wind's not coming up too fast tonight. On her first trip out with LaVon, when he was gathering for his eighteenth year Rites two years ago, she kept gagging on the salt rot of the Atlantic. The wind wouldn't let up, just kept blowing at their faces like it knew death was all they could smell even when they weren't on the mud.

Back then, Harbour had only seen the Atlantic from a distance. Blue, grey-green ocean hitting Fundy red land and spitting up rainbows of trash reminded her of the illustrations of fantasy lands LaVon's friend Ocean showed her at the library when she was just a little kid.

Usually for Rites people take a solo trip out through the mud, but LaVon took Harbour because the dying season was bad that year and he could barely walk from grief. His partners, Ocean and Kit, died during the heatwave that sweeps through right before his summer birthday, yearly. During the heatwave if the winds lift, there's nothing to do to get away from the stench. It colonizes everything, a reminder of casualties. LaVon, Ocean, and Kit dreamt of coming of age together. Harbour could see it on her older brother's still young round face, then: belief in a future. Less let down than thrown, after their deaths, disappointment altered his momentum. LaVon stepped backwards, followed traces of a collective past he once wished he could escape into the water. Harbour, though, she found herself thinking of escape only in dreams.

Harbour found him gold anyway that day and he got to do his Rites. The old folks taught him all the arcane histories that weren't spoken of with children, except in whispers or subtle implications.

When he reappeared on the stone steps of the community centre he looked so shrunk. He lifted his lip with a frail finger to prove his belonging to tradition that now lived in his mouth, a gold canine that would only ever see daylight this once. Harbour didn't know until later how badly whatever Rites taught him had broken his brain. Now she's doing hers—she just wants to know what he learned that left him muttering to himself in their home and walking down to this rotten water to swim until its poison began to eat away at his skin.

Harbour's birthday is at the beginning of the first chill, just after the dying season. A good time to fish for metals out here in the Mud. With the coming hurricanes the waters churned up more of the buried treasures that rested at their depths among the usual Barbies and corpses.

Rocks cut sharp with tiny barnacles. Knees scraped, drawing blood. A particularly bad slip leaves the back of her leg torn. Blood drawn finds Harbour hoping it at least feeds the little white shells something healthy. It's an elementary lesson that barnacles only eat plankton. But it's an elementary lesson too that injury deserves compassion.

Off the rocks, into the mud. Critters slide against her legs, nibbling their dinner from dead skin. Nothing too dangerous here, only a couple parasite reports this year and Harbour is pretty sure the foolish hosts slid a lot deeper than she's planning on going in tonight. Probably they were somewhere they weren't supposed to be and picked up unwanted guests, too embarrassed at breaking the rules to admit their faults to their doctors. Even with all his swimming out here, LaVon hadn't picked anything up. Or, if he had, he'd used his old medical training to deal with it discreetly, avoided contagion, contact with more hosts. He would not pass anything on. Harbour wishes he would pass some things on—but whatever's left of the brother who cared for her as she grew up is gone.

She wades forward, moving plastics aside. The tiny metal detector in her pocket beeps lazily as she steps and scans, steps and scans for any metals she can use for Rites.

Some believe the people in this town are blessed and that's why so much old wealth ends up on their shores. *Over 600 years we were cursed until we found this shore!* The most zealous folk bring out their signs and songs to church on Sunday nights. These aren't the stories Harbour is interested in. Mumma used to talk about a day when she was a kid and all the beach was gold, silver, glimmering with old wealth that didn't mean anything to anyone anymore. It was all washed away in the next day's tides. She never saw a thing like that again but she swears it happened. Harbour would ask: "How come nobody else seen it, then?"

Why didn't she think to keep the gold chain her mother gave her instead of coming all the way out here to scavenge? Careless with her history, possessions. Just gave it to the first person with a pretty voice to lean her way. Would Kaya give it back to her now that they were calling things quits and Harbour needed the gold? It would be too low, even for Harbour, to ask for the chain back. That chain did not mean belonging, no matter how bad she wanted it to. She resented herself for even posing the question.

A strong, fast beep. Harbour's jolted out of her own head. She reaches her gloved hand down into the mud, digs around. Old mussel shell. Water bottle caps. And a thin, gritty, slimy chain. Aha. What she wants. She begins pulling only to meet resistance. It must be stuck on something down there. Try not to pull too hard—*exert force and equal force will confront you*, isn't that what the old folks said in school? So, gentle, gently, as she tries to teach herself to be in this world, she pulls, wraps the necklace chains stuck to necklace chains—a never ending clusterfuck of metal around her neck. Ache of biceps... she wishes she thought to bring wire cutters to break the chain. They had cutters last time.

Still more comes. With no moon to mark the sky it's hard to tell how much time has passed. Endless loops around her neck weigh her to a stoop. Untenable for the trip back. Some perfect things have to be let go. Harbour drops her hands, lets the chains slither out, one long glimmering snake in her mind, caught and released. Like magic, her wonder and terror imagine it to life: the chain keeps slithering deeper, faster. Someone must be at the other end pulling. No wonder it was so hard. Someone out here on the same scavenge as her, some birthday twin out here preparing for their eighteenth Rites.

The chain begins to tighten around her throat. She

calls out, "If you're out there, stop pulling. I'll look for another chain, no worries. Take this one."

The silence that answers is thick as the mud that cradles her feet.

Mumma's voice whispers its way all the way from childhood into Harbour's ear. Tells her there are worse things than parasites and competitive scavengers out here. Worse things she'd seen washed up. Angel's corpses, or whatever it was called when their bodies were so mangled that they could no longer mimic our forms. Sandwiched between the superstition and trauma of living through the aftermath of the last migration she forgot to listen to this truth before it forced its way to her remembrance.

Harbour scrambles to flick her emergency flashlight on, wishing her numb cold fingers could feel. Even when she manages to get it on she can only see the reddish muck within a two metre radius. Her heart shocks the mud on beat. Drops the flashlight and it sinks with her only light. Tries to pull off the chains wrapped foolishly over her shoulders and neck. These chains are no longer decorative lace, just neck metal. Noose. Coffle. Dead ancestor words. It's too tight. She can't pull it over her head. Before Harbour can call out again it's choking her, pulling her deep through the silken mud. She's just another creature hoping to be scavenged from this mucky grave. It's not any darker under here than above. Black as the moon.

MEMBRINGS

Nan said,

Backintheday we wore grillz to represent bringing wealth back to the community.
Backintheday people took our tradition and sold it back to us.
And then, the world ended and we ended up out here alone, those of us who couldn't flee the flood. We thrived. Bloomed like we couldn't in the chaos of resource hoarding and local environmental destruction. This new world wasn't so different from the old-new world or even the plain old world. Violence was taken out of the equation when the people who sewed it fled up to the sky to escape the heat, disease, ocean, cold, and deterioration. The only violence left was what nature inflicted on us. And that's an understanding violence. A needful violence. Many of the old folks of this land stayed. Those of us who came to this land unwillingly, or made peace with being here, or weren't born here by choice in the first place, all stayed. We didn't leave here because we were nurtured by being left alone for once. We weren't liberated; we were left alone, together. And so, the first to receive her Rites

was me: I was one of the youngest adults who had seen the discord that came before our survival. One of the youngest to make and hold space for our communities to move through responsibility to each other. And so we wanted to show how we'd given back to this long-standing crossroads of communities of survival. My moment was helping refugees from up and down the south-eastern coast land on our harbour…

The old folks melted down my mother's gold teeth to fit my mouth instead.

Here, Nan would pop out her grillz and wipe the spit from them, show it to Mumma, who would show Harbour the action by popping out her own grillz to hand it to LaVon who would hand it to Harbour so she could look up close. The gold is thin, a root system that gathers at the gum.

Roots reach forward and back. The ocean can leach them of nutrients, and move those nutrients elsewhere, let them land back on some different shore.

PROPHET

After I wrap Harbour up and her breathing steadies I fall into bed. Where you fill my dreams with images of *car after car after car rushing by these streets, car after car with its sweet gasoline in my nose car after car carrying creatures from place to place, car after car from beginning to end and past both carriages and satellites, core to stratosphere, further and further across the boundaries of space and time. All the engines coughing their last breaths. Death too, to electronics, never electrons.* I wake with a motor between my ears and my feet roll across the pavement. You've instilled me with a fear of water, else my engine breaks down, the mud too slick, I'm sinking until I can break the connection with Harbour's name chanted again and over.

You tell me she slipped under the surface easily. My prophecy, my end. I know you want to take her for yourself. You've called us humans selfish, though you have also called me not human since we touched and you infected my brain with your transmissions. Harbour, you say, is resilient. She is where you must land safely if I refuse. Your sky logic tells you to keep consuming, even after me.

Didn't I let you want me first and enough?

And I'm swimming with my wheels and all my doors shut but I'm heat seeking so I know where you thought about chaining her neck to the ocean floor. I'm working against you, with you: my plan for obsolescence.

You told me I was history and what comes after. Some off-planet satellite owns all our bodies. Like those myths of reality TV. Like theories of existence pieced together by people who haven't experienced being many things at once.

All our conversations transmit and receive until it's one big mess and we're all tangled seaweed. I am you and you are me, sometimes.

You rise out of the water to face me. You look something like human. Something more than you have, in murk. Something like Harbour, having embraced her. Your skin regrows dewy and soft, approximating her deep brown. Stiller, duller, you cannot take her all in. You walk towards me like she would. Everything's slicked with red mud. Red sky.

"Why did you take her?" we ask each other in one voice.

"We own your bodies," you say. Then, to explain as if you haven't already, one thousand times without words: "You don't know your bodies' value."

A fallacy from a tired past. "No," I tell you. We hold onto each other's necks but as we are somewhat one it is impossible to kill you. Eternal circuit of murderous bent. I'm not angry. But you need to die, I think, or change.

All my anger slipped out of me the first time I saw the room where things end for us, surrounded by others drowning in their own bodies. What's your take on death? Or do you even know death, being from up somewhere safe where holy immortality was the way.

Why did I ever want to go to heaven? Why did I ever want a better life? Our poisoned soil was bought and paid for by the people who possess your water-dwelling carcass, who filled it with ideas about whose bodies should survive. Preserve some base from the superstructure above the acid rain, neutralize conflict and fill me with hallucinations of the past.

These moments of clarity are rare. With your hands around my neck you push me under the surface. I'm drinking oil and water and plastic and blood.

Taste of obsolescence, sweet, like gasoline. Then, your hands loosen. It's the bug in your system. You don't realize we are both becoming

HOW HE USED TO BE

Backintheday LaVon took his little baby sister to Library on weekends. She climbed on his back and he gripped her knees, didn't even breathe hard on the uphill climb. When she got too old to be carried he'd fill her book bag with everything they'd borrowed and sling it over his own back, so she could run unencumbered out in front of him and wave back, yelling at him to catch up with the lisp of missing teeth. He didn't even breathe hard on the uphill with all these books on his back: a book about what hid beyond the clouds, one about cooking, another about herbs, one about swimming that he didn't intend to return yet, and tools: a hammer, some sheers. A personal loan: Ocean's knife.

Seven days of working hard nursing before this trip to the library, he'd come home beat. Harbour noticed the tightness in his jaw, his smile enforced strict borders. Beginning of the dying season and he talked of saving lives. "No one has died yet this year." But they would in time. He smiled at the good, was hungry for the mussels in broth that Harbour had perfected just for him. Even after these long weeks he couldn't wait to get down to the library to talk to Ocean about what it was like to make sure everyone had what they needed. This was his purpose, his tank of endless fuel—to care, to heal.

Harbour left him for the other kids as soon as they crossed the library's threshold. Couldn't hear, but watched as his face filled with the sun reflecting off his special friend. After Harbour, the only person who could make him glow like this was Ocean, showing off her knife tricks and newly refurbished books. Ocean could make him hold his breath for the entire length between their visits, making him sigh at her insistence to bring things back to the library on time. Said she'd teach him how to swim in a ravine she found. Told him water is nothing to fear, else why'd her parents give her this name?

He'd grin goofy the whole way home and pull Harbour into dancing with him at church. Even with his too big shoes that clomped all over her feet, she couldn't say no to her big brother lifting her into the air, saying "This is what we were made for—"

He could have meant anything, but there was Ocean waving across the room. And there was that shepherd Kit waving to LaVon again.

Inevitable sleep took her, leaning against someone's scratchy wool sweater on a bench. The pattern pasted on her face, he would find her and pull her soft, floppy body over his shoulder, carry her all the way home. He tucked her in good, just like Mumma did, just like she would for him when he got sick and lost everyone except her and did his Rites and all that was left of him was the tiniest twinkle of fool's gold in the corner of his eye.

NEW TOOTH

First time really awake in a week, Harbour stands in front of the mirror, lifts her tongue with salty fingers. The muscle is slippery, boa constrictor strong. It relaxes between index and forefingers. She looks down her nose into the mirror, up her nostrils, and the larger cavern below, gaping mouth. She gazes into the basin of her lower jaw. The lightning reserve powered light in their bathroom is dim. To find the right tilt to see below her tongue, to find the itchy-pain that's lived there since LaVon found her misplaced on a bed of plastics and seaweed, she must stretch into discomfort. Tongue in fingers makes this tongue an object outside of herself. This mouth upon waking feels not her own. Inseparably strange.

A glint, a new white spark like a piece of forgotten hard-boiled eggshell. Or was it something more iridescent? The rainbow skim of oil over the Kennebecasis's fresh water a few times a year. It's so pure and smooth-looking that Harbour drops her tongue from my fingers so she can feel over it, around its erupting ridges.

The closer she leans the more warped her reflection becomes in the liver-spotted glass. With her weight against the sink, the house's useless pipes creak. This old house that's survived so many injuries needs a gentleness Harbour often lacks.

She pokes the bud. Her best new tooth. It wobbles in its gum-embedded shrine. Tiny, there, hiding, almost a gift to remind her of her own precarity, leaking blood that feeds her the tangy taste of drowning in the ocean.

Similar as they are in taste, blood is not saltwater; it's more comforting. Something of its thickness.

"What you looking at?" he asks.

Pulls away, snaps jaw shut. It's rare LaVon speaks to her. Her lips stick to the air-dried stickiness of the gumskin. LaVon's skeletal face is a poor copy of what it was two years ago. She never tells him this, but it splinters her constantly. Harbour looks between his eyes just above the bridge of his nose so she never has to see how his eyes have become like old marbles. "Nothing. Looking where I'm going to put my grillz after Rites."

His head tilts, bottom lip juts. "Hm."

Harbour asks: "Did I have any gold on me? When you found me?" Did the chain that wrapped itself around her neck leave any souvenirs, or only bruises?

Head shakes: *no*. He shuffles to grab his toothbrush from its place in the cup. Harbour smells of the ocean, putrid. LaVon smells like a dead man. Worse.

"I'm going to the baths to wash off the ocean. Want to come?"

Head shakes: *no*. The only time her brother will let water touch his body is if he's swimming. *Bathing doesn't feel like swimming* is what he keeps telling Harbour. She knows bathing and swimming aren't the same. One is for getting clean. She wishes she could pull him up the hill to care for himself, even if he kicked and screamed the whole way. Wouldn't it make him feel better? Bringing it up now isn't worth the frustration of trying to fight with a wall of silence.

"I have to go back for more gold. Can you come?" Doesn't want to admit she's so terrified she's considered abandoning her Rites, even if that means never knowing the full truth of her little world. If she had some help from her brother to allay her fears and provide some caution, another trip could work out.

On the mud caution is smart; fear is deadly. She's not sure either of them could survive her almost drowning again. If there was another way than the mud, if Kaya would give the chain back—
She must do her Rites. Fear or not. She needs to know whatever her brother saw that melted his brain into some other someone.

He nods: *yes*. She hugs his limp torso. His arms don't wrap around Harbour's. He connects at brittle joints. Strange to think his body moves its way through water easily as a shark.

"You don't drown like normal," her brother whispers in her ear. Harbour runs her tongue over her new tooth. It's not the kind that indicates wisdom. It is something else entirely. She passes by LaVon's decaying body. The baths will bring some normal to this strange day.

ALIEN FALLING

There is a difference between what it is and what the angels were:

It survives. To become something else on the seafloor

After it falls it gets lonely so

It makes sense of the Atlantic, maps host-bodies onto its consciousness, builds a little compassion out of dead matter

And loses it when the storms leave no room to resist violent motion. It fell slowly enough to make beauty before its crash to new home. Old home never really felt

Right. Equations of humanity too complicated. Much easier to make a myth of survival and live inside it with everyone else

Its arrival might signal a return, someday to that sky, to that easy life, if it can build itself a way out, if this is not all that's left, if it can use a body to become more, to become what it was programmed to be, to supersede earth, to exit into the stars and live on through abandonment

It holds its prophet dear and tight around the neck. Their temporal desperations align them in life beneath the surface

It needs to take shape. it needs to take

to become something else

It transmits:

VENUS AT THE BATHS

Harbour inches the wood door closed, lifts its iron handle firmly so the door doesn't stick and shriek goodbye to her jumpy brother. Better not drag him along. Besides, she hopes she'll catch a glimpse of Kaya.

Every three days she heads out early, leaves her shadow imprinted on the fog, temporary as light burned to retinas—a feeling she knows from the rare occasions of sun she savours. Sleep fades from her body, slow too. Sleep and fog and light, all pushed aside in the warmth of the bathhouse.

Others are here early. Regulars, old folks. People whose eyes Harbour doesn't mind catching on her unseen angles. If willing, they exchange hellos with mouths and bare skin. This way, they understand the community's bodies better, their scars and seams visible as they aren't in marketplace or church. But in all their tired faces and bodies she doesn't see who she wants.

Before the final door to the bathwater she pauses. This is either a door to disappointment or relief.

Relief: Kaya, who was usually here by routine before things went sour between them a couple weeks back. Before Harbour made herself too present in Kaya's life and was met with coldness. She should be here today, waiting and seen.

Dim light of dawn leaks through the high windows. This place was a cathedral. Now, it's used to worship differently. Everyone's eyes half closed. Water almost too hot. Steam doubles as a veil here, gives privacy, marks people as individuals. Makes it harder to look at others, to focus on anything but your own cleanse. But Harbour is in her orbit: Kaya slips over and under the surface of the bathwater, pulling her hair through with a wide tooth chitin comb. Massages oil from tips to scalp and back again. Scent of rosemary, lavender, and flax transmitted over steam.

She has the cool tones of Venus about her. Harbour saw them once, swirling around Kaya when she sang at church in the woods behind the community centre: bright blues, purple-greens, crushed between more ambient shades and hints of dusty browns: the clean sheen on a bubble, a pearl.

Harbour and Kaya spoke for the first time since their school days six months ago after service. They drank dandelion wine and Kaya told Harbour she knew who she was even though they'd never spent any meaningful time together. Harbour rolled her eyes and Kaya denied that this was some corny past soulmates bullshit. This was a knowing like how listening makes sense of sound. It was easy for her to know Harbour without being told. Intriguing when Harbour didn't feel the same. Didn't know Kaya, only knew that it was the not knowing that drew almost everyone in, and fucked them all over in the end, when they realized what they felt wasn't love but possessiveness. And Kaya thought she knew that in the end Harbour was just the same. Was she just the same? Or was Kaya bored?

Either way, it was over because Kaya said so.

Still, Harbour thinks of the Renaissance like it was yesterday when she sees Kaya slip back into the water. She didn't know about the other Venus until Mumma told her. The Venus that's not a planet. Mumma had an art book, discoloured from water damage, but still legible. Harbour would trace the shell beneath the long-haired woman and wonder how she sprang more fully formed than any mollusk could ever be. Why did the others in the image want to cover her? Consume her? She didn't understand why the darkest of them was light brown skinned and yet all of them were out in the midday sun.

"The sun didn't burn so much backintheday," Mumma explained. A world where even the lightest skinned could sit out on nice days, let the rays catch the angles of their bodies that were often left in shadow.

Kaya: some brown skinned rural Venus, born from a shell.

Those who were there remember baby Kaya arriving from the ocean on the doorstep of a flood. Raised here, she was never quite claimed as the town's own. She is ethereal and otherly. A trace of myth follows her still. Or maybe that's all talk. Harbour knows Kaya wants to leave it behind.

Looking is frowned upon here. Harbour turns her back. Worries new tooth with her tongue. Brush water over salty body. Dips head under. *Ah*. Brushes out braids and massages scalp. In all she has to brush it through eight times before the sand is all out, dropped around her feet.

Tiny waves grate Harbour's skin as Kaya steps out of the Bath. Her absence leaves the water wanting. Harbour is surprised and pleased to see the gold chain she gifted to Kaya months ago still glints around her ankle. Souvenir of a moment when Harbour didn't care that they might not be forever. Would she give it back if Harbour asked nice? Wouldn't it be easier to ask her for the chain then go back to the edge of the water where she almost drowned, her sick brother in tow?

Kaya lifts herself out of the water. It falls around her, perfect teardrops. She disappears around the corner to the change room. Harbour lets her eyes droop closed like the rest of the people in the Baths. She pretends privacy. Wishes that Kaya had looked at her instead of passing her eyes over her without recognition again and again, even when she looked back passing her eyes over Harbour's face and revealed nothing of knowing.

WALK HOME

Through the Baths' steam, Harbour's watching was more about longing than longing to know. Kaya is thinking of leaving or else she might have returned Harbour's dishonest stare of unfinished romance.

Recently, this longing to know has been turning Kaya's head away from want. An itch to get outside these borders she's accidentally grown up between. Baby delivered on contaminated water, motherless. Still can't find her place in the harmony of this town.

Harbour! Damn dandelion wine, damn desire. Damn her searching lips and moony eyes parting the mist at the baths to find her. Damn all the lust she can't scrub from her skin. Damn the blood beneath, its pulsing melody of want, frustration of loss heating her feverish, pitches of regret drone on: should've gone to see Harbour after she nearly drowned
even after ending things between them
can't stand Harbour's ability to moor her
that Kaya wants to be moored
should've asked
what it's like beneath the surface

should've asked if Harbour wanted to come with her which would've been selfish. Forget belonging together, here. Kaya's choice to leave is the only thing left that makes her feel herself and not some half-forgotten legend dogged by her own shadow.

Kaya crests the last hill before home to watch the fog burn off in its red-orange haze. Hums against boredom watching the sun's brief cut through the curtain. Fights with herself not to look away and miss the moment of brightening. Loses, as always. Heads home.

She's lost interest in this patch of purgatory. Soon she'll disappear like dust wiped from an otherwise blank surface.

Then, there she is again, standing outside the co-op house, watching her bike sit unused, leaning against the side of the house's peeling sideboards. She thinks about riding over potholed roads north until tout le monde parle français and she only understands fragments. If there's even anyone left up there.

If the place where she was raised is home then this

is hers. Endless turnover of parentless youth. She's now the eldest. Supposed to manage it all but she does so sloppily, rarely takes responsibility. The majority of the labour falls on Faith, who says she doesn't mind since she knows Kaya is busy with her songwriting, practicing, performing at church on Sundays… It must bother Faith a little. It bothers Kaya that she isn't better at caring for these parentless kids, or even capable of providing herself with the care she was lucky to receive as an orphaned child. These peeling walls bore her so deeply. All the loss concentrated in these walls is so boring and unforgivable. She doesn't come from the same place. She was cut off from whoever her people were supposed to be up in that sky she so rarely sees.

She mumbles hello to all the people splayed on threadbare couches and carpets tossing around cards and jokes before she shuffles to the kitchen. Pretends not to see everything, who is fucking who is caring for who is feeding who is loving is hating is making whose life better/worse/stable/forgettable/memorable or whatever is in between all that.

Beans and molasses wait bowled for her next to the stove. Considerate and caring Faith, so deeply not family, though the youngest children might see her this way. Why doesn't she ever return the favour of care? Ungrateful in the almost warm of almost belonging to a place… What's wrong with her?

Kaya takes the beans up to her room.

Faith is asleep in Kaya's bed instead of her own, down the hall, mouth open, drooling deep sleep all over Kaya's best pillowcase. Her after-breakfast nap. She's washed the sheets since last night. Scraps of lyrics surround Faith's torso. One crushed beneath her armpit, pokes gently between her hairs. Kaya's musician fingers feel for the weak spots on her legs. Crook of the knee. Terminally ticklish, Faith wakes immediately, throws herself to the crumby floor. Pretends to fall back asleep, laughs at Kaya's serious face.

Off again, on again, Faith slept in Kaya's bed last night. Her post hookup clinginess makes Kaya's teeth grind in frustration. She has to break it off. Weren't they better as friends? If there's any whiff of romance Kaya didn't catch it. All of a sudden Faith doesn't understand boundaries, privacy, intimacy, any of it. She loves Kaya. Kaya loves Faith. But maybe not like that. Soon she'll be out of this town.

"I need the room to practice. Music night tonight."

As polite as Kaya can be about it, she pulls at Faith's shoulder a bit. Gentle let down. Had Faith expected to spend the morning together?

"You always play the same thing. Can't you just leave it and lie next to me for today?" If she'd wanted to, maybe. She doesn't want to.

Kaya moves to the corner as she lifts herself back onto my bed. Grabs her guitar, feels cool relief trickle across her over-stoked body. A relief she doesn't feel lying next to Faith, as much as it's nice. As much as they grew up together and know each other's different fucked up losses in and out.

Faith knows something is different with her. Knows desire grates on Kaya, tries to hide her joy and act mechanic when they touch. Easy enough. It's after that's hard, when she starts to hear Faith humming a tune that she's plucking out on her guitar, that Kaya is sure she'll never be able to give Faith what she needs. Kaya needs to leave Faith and all her goodness in this home to grow.

"I have some new stuff I want to work on."

"Can I listen?"

No more pretending. "Please leave." No apology. Regrets immediately the hurt reddening across Faith's cheeks.

"You think I don't get it about you and Harbour but I do." Faith's hair kelp-flops in front of her face to hide whatever shyness she has at the chance of this turning into a fight. "You don't want her to know your emptiness. I know your emptiness and still love you. Can't you see that?" Kaya doesn't challenge Faith. Uncomfortable with silence she follows up: "Can you do the dishes later?"

"Yeah."

Kaya turns away, fingers the guitar until it warms its strings. Faith gathers her things and leaves. Kaya ignores her hurt, feels around the perimeter of the gold chain Harbour clasped around her ankle. She can't find the seam where it connects, as much as she looks. Gives up, riffs a little bit. It sounds out:
nothing
nothing
nothing
new.

TRANSMISSIONS

Once Harbour is out for the day, I walk down to the cove and drop into the ocean.

Watch, slowly: these images you send my brain, settling in air. I settle back into the water's skin and it settles
into mine. I'm a good listener. You think it's because I'm careful. It's not. It's because I hold the air tight and close, breathe warmth into it with my diaphragm, give it life, let myself become part of the sounds made by membranes as they bump and mesh.

At the bottom of this uncanny cove there is no life but me—and I am barely life. You might consider "life" to be something with a beating heart if you come from before, when the definition of life was a narrow-minded collection of criteria. I am barely life and the voices that sound from this bed of sea-battered detritus are a different kind of barely life than I am, even. Lying on this bed the lives that came before speak to me if I let them in.

I wait and I wait until they speak. Tell of futurity launched from the past:

These oceans stopped rising with water but keep rising with plastics and memories.

A plastic water bottle tells me about a family eaten away from cancer before their taps would spit anything but scum and fire.

Bagsandbagsandbagsandbags drift, flat fishes in the water, where plant life was, where other bags were, where more bags and bags and bags will be and bags and bags and bags are swimming in schools stuck together by bags and forks and knives and straws and rope in long dragons of bags that surface only to scare people into believing the oldest stories.

They never thought we'd survive. We as in life but we as in the children of our ancestors in general.

I ask questions to the people in the water that you consume and haunt:

How did you think I was born here?

They answer:

From survival or luck.

How did we get here?

By accident, with song.

Did you think we would?

Never.
Yes.
We were unprepared for the prospect of continued life after the midcentennial collapse.

I ask questions to you, in your future:

How many days can I stay inside in the dark before I lose my humanity?

How many stitches will bind the two halves of my brain together before they leak from my skull to the ground?

How many people know what I know; that they could be cured of illness, even the common sickness? That for angels, death didn't exist anymore, barring injury, such as falling from the sky and breaking across the ocean's crust. For angels, the people who made you, the people you were a part of before falling and becoming alien, for the people who left us, disease was something to cure.

And when I can't hold my breath waiting for your answers anymore, the air tells me what the water can't. It speaks with words in jumbled paragraphs I often can't parse. I repeat it back, hoping for understanding. Maybe what you want is simple nothing.

And still, I'll wait even in the night when I'm lying still on an itchy bed of wool, curtains drawn, Harbour snoring beside me, and listen for your call:

CROSSROADS

Wasn't it good? Those first few months of undressing slowly, a performance of devotion neither Kaya nor Harbour could sustain.

Their sweet and sloppy hearts exchanged hands, Harbour clenched tighter until the juice ran from her fingers and Kaya's chest began to ache. Kaya forgot Harbour's heart back home. Left it out on her dresser where it lost moisture, grew dry and cracked.

"Stay longer, stay later." Harbour and Kaya pull each other close before it's time to walk down to the community centre to ask for their Rites. Harbour is welcomed, Kaya refused. They don't know if they would work for her. She lets her disappointment hibernate behind the aching, sloshy hole in her torso. Harbour can't help buzzing in her ears with big relief, anticipation for Rites, showing off her soon to be decorated teeth, tugging on the gold chain that hangs from her neck with her tongue, sucking on it to acclimate to the taste of metal in her mouth.

Kaya breaks things off. Until this point, their lives had run parallel in his town. Now that they've crossed paths, a deadline for their split is set. Harbour will be wedded to this place. Kaya relegated to singing its anthems without tasting belonging. Belonging's been dead for a while now, she was just lapping up the leftovers.

Harbour says Kaya belongs with her. Says she'll find some other gold than this chair, gifts it to represent Kaya's value to her. Wasn't value supposed to have died too, with the rest of the old world? Maybe she is some resurrection. Some bad omen. She wants to love but can't forget the limits of her own strangeness, how much everyone she knows wants her to stay something they cannot fear.

All of this must end.

She leaves Harbour behind and walks to the shore to look to the sky, her origin. Above her, a patch of blue. She wills herself to levitate. Cannot.

In the distance she spots LaVon. He climbs over a pink and blue trash dune and without once looking back, slips into the rhythm of the waves.

GOLD DESIRES

People don't go out much at night. The old folks in the town perpetually lust for some pastime that might let them use the momentum of a good night out for the stormy weeks ahead. Just past sunset on Sundays, at the clearing behind the community center, the town gathers in a tight circle around whoever brings their song and calls this church. Song brings everyone who survived this many years past the end of life here, and it will keep on pushing them into the future. Song itself is at the root of all survival.

Feeding that root is Kaya. She holds the momentum of the town, momentarily, when she leads the circle for ten or fifteen minutes. She sings her way into songs she had never heard except hummed on the backdraft of a passerby. They grace her. As she falls into each melody her back is tight but her voice is open. It allows for some mundane transcendence—a transcendence not so far away from baking a perfect loaf of bread, seeing a rare fish leap from the water, or the reappearance of an old earring behind a dresser. It's the only kind of transcendence that exists since all the survivors of the lost earth migrated to this strange corner or else vaulted into the sky. Harbour needs the thin gold chain that drips as temptingly as honey onto the sharp ridges of Kaya's foot. It's sedimented itself in her flesh, fossilized, lost sweetness. In the end of things Harbour knew Kaya would have returned the chain to her willingly—Kaya had tried many times to return it to Harbour, knotted and thrust warm from her angry palms. But how could she take back what she gave? If she asked for it back, she'd let the clasp of their time together snap, breaking all that had made her feel whole, all that wholeness that still might come. It might. Kaya might change her mind about Harbour in time.

But now she needs the chain more than the stale crumbles of Kaya's promise to know her. She can imagine no deeper shame than asking for the thing she gifted back. But nearly drowning left Harbour with only desperation rooted in survival instincts. She cannot slog through the mud again.

Harbour concedes that she may have misunderstood the purpose of gifting. Something inside forces her to view giving in terms of getting even before the giving is done. Any of her belongings might be rented out for a good-feeling in her chest. Is it wrong, this feeling? She doubts its rightness, but still, it cramps her heart, undeniable as a craving. She polishes the smooth new tooth sprouting from her jaw with worry.

The chain she'd placed around Kaya's ankle so that it could linger and languish there, making their love permanent where it settled. It left a thin tanline in the summer, an umber imprint beneath socks in winter.

When it really comes down to it, Harbour doesn't know if she can prevent the toxic spread of a hoarder's sort of possessiveness across her brain. Once she knows she wants something she *knows*.

She wants.

As a child she would hoard the fruit she picked with the rest of her classmates on Tuesdays and Thursdays in Agriculture and Community class. Seasonally affected preference for blueberries, apples, pigeon berries, gathered in flats, or else large mesh bags stacked in a corner of the pantry where her Mumma would berate her for bringing too much home, more than anyone could eat. The rot would begin its spread. She hated to eat the fruits. She just liked the security of having them there in case.

She'd force herself to eat the rest of the blueberries, apples, pigeon berries, sometimes until she felt sick. She'd watch Kaya walk back and wish she hadn't walked up the hill to give the chain back and apologize the last time they fought. Why did Kaya keep wearing the chain if it did not mean Love or Attachment or Futurity? Or was it fear, that unlooking, that undoing, unsharing, unwillingness to accept that Harbour wants her?

Was this some sort of disorder of the mind that was becoming rarer as years went by? Why her, why was she so afflicted with it? She knows possessiveness made the old world crumble. She still can't stop wanting. Wanting foolish things mostly. Kaya.

When what she needs is her brother.

Kaya is not wealth.

Wealth does not equal survival.
Wealth does not equal survival.

Wealth does not equal survival.
Wealth does not equal survival.
Wealth does not equal survival.
Wealth does not equal survival.

The prayer they'd recite every day before schooling.

She is not survival.

Survival is resistance.
Survival is resistance.
Survival is resistance.
Survival is resistance.
Survival is resistance.
Survival is resistance.

She must resist.

Where was the space between?

Harbour can't own that gold once it is given. She can't melt it down and wear it over her teeth until she dies. She will have to go back to the mud. Even if she asks for it back out of desperation, she would always see it where she had first wanted to: dangling off Kaya's ankle to remind her that nothing was hers, not even desire.

Kaya's voice rises the tides on the nights she sings. There might well be no future beyond this moment.

But tonight something breaks. Not her voice. Harbour's face is screwed with the intent of trying to loosen the chain tight around Kaya's delicate ankle as if telekinetically. When she gifted it to Kaya, Kaya was told to keep it locked where it is now. She'd accepted its place.

An unwelcome distraction. Everyone in town is tired of fights between ex-lovers. Move on. We're all we got. If you don't like what you've got, find something else. If Kaya could, she'd take Harbour down to the water and throw her far from shore. So far that she would stop interrupting this evening with her desire. Kaya's vocals rub harshly against the clumsy dance of her fingers over sharp metal strings turning the harmonic resonance dull. Whatever momentary ecstasy she incited in the community is past. And Kaya is dragged back to an unwelcome past too. She burns from the friction, toward the pull Harbour exerts on the thin chain, toward whatever story Harbour has constructed about belonging. Belonging together.

It's whiny and childish but Kaya says it anyway when the song is done: "Stop looking at me like that." The type of thing she would've said to Faith across the breakfast table at seven years old. And in front of everyone. Whatever rare pleasure she'd felt at the familiarity of community is shattered. This is bad behaviour in public, no one has the time for anything but pleasure. Isn't that what Kaya is for?

"I'm not looking at you." Harbour's voice is different, like her tongue's wrapped in burrs and it's sticking in her mouth. "I need it back." Kaya used to love its softness in her ears. Now it wraps around her ankle and tugs the chain. Of course, she cared about Harbour. People talked about how she didn't go visit after the drowning because she didn't care, but she cared as much as she would have cared if anyone in the co-op house had nearly drowned. She should've gone. But it was too soon. Visiting would have felt too much like paying off emotional debt. It's not her fault Harbour couldn't handle things ending like a regular person and just suck it up, fuck someone else, or something up, at the very least. Maybe it's easier to pay up whatever perceived debt has incurred now even if Kaya doesn't think there is anything to pay off at all—better to give back a chain than her heart. Nobody has the luxury of giving their heart away except in stories about backintheday. And yet, Harbour wants it anyway.

Kaya sets her guitar on the moss. The strings twang moodily at being left behind. Their resonance evokes a new song borne of resentment, sucked teeth, deep sighs, and murmured gossip that rises up around Kaya as she walks toward Harbour. All the energy in the room hovers in the space between them. A lifted foot placed on the leg of a chair, the chain unclasped in a violent struggle, dropped in a shimmering gold stream onto Harbour's lap. The chain settles gently over the hills of Harbour's thighs. They jiggle delicately.

Harbour: she thinks herself a river, she thinks herself an ocean, but her name is Harbour and someday she will be swallowed with all the rest of dry land.

When she picks the guitar off the moss and continues with her music, something is flat in the chords of Kaya's voice. The tides barely rise, no one can bring themselves to transcend. People go home early for drinks inside instead. Even Harbour disappears with the crowd, no hanging on to Kaya's ankles now that she holds the chain in her fist.

Last to leave. Kaya heads home alone. Finds Faith slouched at the kitchen table where she knew Faith would be—faithful rebound, Faith. She waited up late among the crumbs to welcome Kaya with a hot drink. The dishes are still piled in the sink where she forgot them. Careless, thoughtless. She can't be in this town anymore where she only expects the worst and can only bring herself to act if it's careless. She can no longer wait.

No more sleeping next to people until she can't tell herself from them. Kaya packs a bag, leaves a note, then leaves herself. Whistles only one note before she remembers that in letting herself become forgotten in this place, silence is necessary.

CREATION MYTHS

echo in its cavities. No gilgamesh, jesus, strange relationship to water nonetheless

how did it find itself here? It's more of a factory build, lab test, shipwrecked survivor of falling skies. Resting 'til it finds the right vessel to spike with capital. Its prophet sees its coming as neutral. Its coming is survival

Again and again. Resistance as breathing. Not that it breathes. It knows breathing. Speaking to the fishes brings it no joy that land life could. Aquatic futures rest between the ridges of its skin. 20 years submerged and rising

Memory hits a wall. After a while it finds refuge in the present. Perhaps it is looking in the wrong places to understand how it fell. Perhaps it came from the sea and not the sky. They are so close together when one calculates to a larger scale than these humans do

Even as a transportable ecosystem it finds itself lastly considered. First of its kind on earth and seas. Last of its kind in sky

Motor failed, impaled on its own longing for companionship. It is not human. It is not not human. It is not not not not human. I am human? I am not

The prophet comes to it and holds his head above water to watch his history. In all these dead bodies long ago there was no trace of it. In all those dead bodies long ago, a baby who was once a part of it, now left behind and spared of trauma. They protected her. The prophet tells me they named her: Kaya.

She thinks she is human, so she must be. She is not trademarked. She is here accidentally, as it is. As it made her

And then, its prophet tells it, she is gone

SONGLESS

Something tickles the back of Kaya's throat. Her voice disappears over the first hill.

Outside of town she sleeps bundled on a hillside, watching the fog below creep. Where she could see the small movements of town yesterday, she no longer sees anything but thick cloud.

South.

She's headed north.

She snacks on seed loaf and scrabbles the sides of ravines for the better part of a day. Fragments of lyrics dribble down to the bottom of the ravine, soundless. When she makes it to the top, the tuneless wind whistles in her ears.

Up here is a blueberry barren. She picks and nibbles until the sun begins to set. Her fingers are dead girl blue. She has to take her air filter scarf off to eat the berries. The air is thick, but not with smog. The trees around this barren are stripped of their bark. When her stung lungs start to give in, she pulls the scarf over her mouth and heads downhill to find some water to boil. She grabs enough dry sticks to make a small fire. Eating something warm allows her to forget how scared she is out here, alone where she wanted to be.

It's dawn. Something nuzzles her feet. Her eyes are crusted shut. They peel open painfully, eyelashes barring her sight. Something else is breathing deep, loud.

The bear has two heads. Each one hangs low as they turn to face the base of a skeleton tree. She suffocates something between a scream and gasp of wonder. Its fur is blue-black and in patches it has lost pigment. The patches of gold shimmer against the filtered sun. Its species is black bear. *Ursa americanus.* Her species was *homo sapiens sapiens.* Now, both are simple survivors. She looks into their four eyes. They are soft. *Why aren't your eyes soft? All this earth opens to you, and you look at it all hard?* they seem to ask.

Kaya knows she exists back in town only when she sings. Do they miss her? It doesn't matter. The bear passes by, keeps wandering until it disappears into trees.

Further northeast in a few days: she still has not met another town. Today she crosses into the ruin of one. Coastal, like her own. There is still food on the Superstore shelves from 70 years ago. No one has taken any of it. All those stories from the older kids at the co-op house growing up that if you left town limits you'd be attacked, murdered, raped by scavengers who raided the old corporate stores for supplies… of course they weren't true. Or maybe they were true then. The outside world she's entered is, so far, unpopulated by people.

Surveying the shelves, Kaya weighs her options and takes a can of beans, pork, and molasses. It reminds her of home, though she won't admit the missing to herself. Cooks it good over her fire, which she starts in an abandoned house. The flue is clear, the fireplace works. Rats skitter around her feet, not shy of her human presence. All survivors. Standing up on their hind legs they beg her to share. She chokes down half the can and leaves the rest outside.

Rats swarm it instead of her. She sleeps on a mattress covered in a thick layer of dust.

Thoughtless. Eating an ancient can of beans. Anyone would have told her not to. Hot inside and cool skin. Her brain stem melts into jerks and shudders and she vomits until nothing comes up but bile. She still tries to walk but doesn't make it far. She leans against a telephone pole that's leaning against a tree that's leaning into more leaning and she can't stop thinking about if she hadn't lost the goddamn chain she still would've had someone who wanted her back. Maybe belonging wasn't such a bad thing. The chain was heavy enough to keep her tethered to the earth, to town, to people, her people. So silly to resent everyone for seeing her as beautiful, for using her again and again as an instrument to their ends, some middleway for clout, for sex, or satisfaction, how sick it's made her to cut everyone off one by one and sing songs about love into the night, how sick to let this world go on, how sick to care for no one and receive no care in return. How sick to not know where she came from for however many years she's existed, just that she belonged in town and sang the songs and completed some cycle. Who gave her this name? Who gave her this rotten spirit to carry? She might as well die. She might.

She wanders to the edge of the beach. Looking out past all that plastic she can see where she came from, a faraway version of herself rising from the water and smiling, waving.

But somebody reaches and pulls her back. Their hand is cold and wet, like it's been lying on the bottom of the ocean for at least one hundred years. And it feels like kin, doesn't it, to hold hands with death?

ANGELS

Can't leave me behind so Mumma picks Harbour up and wraps her onto her body. Holds my hand all the way down to the water and we smell it before we see it, smell it worse than a dead mouse found behind stove Saturday afternoon when looking for ball wherever it rolled away. Bouncy, bounce, bounce bounce, these bodies bounce bounce bounce up on the tides. We see them now. I see them now. Mumma doesn't close my eyes the way Ocean's parents do, move her back behind the bushes where she sits playing with grass asking "What's that smell?"

"I wanna leave," I tell Mumma.

"Don't look."

I can't not look. Half a man is trailing like seaweed back towards the water in pinks and reds. His skin is ripped. When I get cut even a little bit Mumma kisses it better. No kissing this better.

All the breakfast porridge comes up and I'm crying. At five I know death happens. We all know death happens. I didn't know this kind of destruction happened to bodies.

"Don't look." Mumma presses her hand across my face. We walk closer to the water. Her palm smells like flax oil and for months I can't smell that oil without gagging at the trail that comes with it, trail of ripped guts, punctured faces, toothy disintegration of the body as a whole.

Don't look. Don't look.

Not Harbour crying—another baby. Mumma's hand drops from my eyes to her mouth.

"Whose child is that?"

Everyone says it's no one's child, found between intestine and hair and bladderwrack, all of which look similar. Red-faced and wailing, cradled in a mussel shell so big I could fit in there too, if I curled up, if I tried.

All this. Was it around when I was born too? Mumma says I was born clean in the bathwater. Clean. Wanted to wash myself clean then. Wanted to be home in low light, Mumma singing to me and scrubbing my skin, clean in our yellowed tub. Mumma detangling my hair before bed.

Someone else picks the baby up. One of the old folks. Mumma grips my hand tighter.

"Take your children home," the same elder tells her. "Take yourself home."

"I want to go home," I wail. "Mumma, why are all these mermaids dead?"

Mumma's not moving. The elder takes her shoulder, turns her around, pushes us back toward town. "They're angels, honey," the elder softens their voice and squeezes my shoulder with a firm hand. I turn to get a last look, but they've made themself into a wall behind me.

I don't go near the water again until I see my friends die. It's where all the dead go back to. Where I should get comfortable, with or without you.

RITES

Harbour sleeps with the gold chain in her palm the night before Rites. Since Kaya returned it to her she's kept it in Mumma's old jewelry box in the deep closet she shares with her brother. Inside the box it was cleansed of Kaya's smells and took on Mumma's.

When she wakes, Harbour holds the thin chain to feel its slipperiness through her fingers. The crunch too: metal upon metal. The two ends lock together, a snake who eats its own head.

Today is her Rite Day.

Harbour's desire to receive her Rites is something chemical. She can't make sense of it beyond the possibility of knowing what her brother saw as jittery anticipation. Shouldn't she be sick with dread instead of desire? When others asked after church why she decided to receive Rites she gave a variety of answers: for her age and contributions to the community, teaching the younger kids about this land some weekends, taking people to plant gingkoes where older trees fall, and working on restoring historical houses from the water damaged husks they've become. All these odd jobs and nothing really to say for reasoning. It felt right. She needed to know the histories.

Holding this thin chain she took back from Kaya, she doesn't know if she deserves them, if she's really ready to be part of keeping people good and responsible to each other. Keeping everyone in this place content so that none of them want to leave. Harbour is scared to leave. The old folks tell everyone that death is surely outside of their own harsh yet controlled environment. This is and was home.

None of these thoughts help her get out of bed. Harbour places the chain on the corner of her nightstand. She pushes past her musty covers, and goes to her closet to pick out her clothes. There aren't many options. When she was younger, Harbour read paperbacks where girls her age used to have closets that someone could walk into. Closets that held infinite identities. You could mix and match until you felt you looked like who you were, or who you wanted to be. Sometimes Harbour tucks her shirt differently than is fashionable. When people stare she gets embarrassed and rights herself.

LaVon helped her press and steam her canvas pants. They're just off the black they were supposed to be when she got them passed *down* down. Her blouse is dusty. She hates wearing it. Only wears it when she absolutely must. Shakes it out anyway, over the floor. Motes fall in the dim light. Glances in the mirror, not for too long or else she starts hating everything that reminds her of those she's lost. Sticks Mumma's hoop in her left ear, her birth father's stud in the right. Her hair she pulls back into a ponytail, slow, savouring her fingers' smoothing over the curls, the weight of all her hair pulling her neck back and chin high.

Harbour took this chain from Kaya. She holds it where Kaya's hand is not. Where she wished Kaya's hand was. *It was mine to begin with.* One last childish thought before she severs her links to the past and takes responsibility today.

"LaVon?"

He stirs. Places his pillow over his head.

"How do I look for my Rites."

He mumbles something into his pillow. "Alright." It sounds like. Or "Alive." Which is true, and ideal in her case.

Harbour takes the long way to the community centre.

Definitively, she notices, the seasons have turned. This morning a congestion of fog greys everything and only burns off for about an hour in the afternoon to leave a thickness of sooty clouds. No rain falls. There is only the anticipation of wetness. Bread grows a fur coat. Bedsheets are musted and itchy.

Harbour's breath wades shallow in her chest, mouth dries, teeth stick on her lips and cheeks. She enters through heavy metal doors. The six old folks sit along the back wall, sharing stories and laughing loud. Nothing to be nervous about. Harbour drops her chain before the Ritegivers, none of whom are strangers—no one in town is—but strange and unknowable in this context. All of them wear shifting faces.

After formal reintroductions, everyone drinks mushroom tea and together they slip into a separate world. Stomach ache, pulsing walls, pulsing skin. Shaved head bristling, sharp as glitter, hooked up to the brainstem simulator Harbour falls into history. At this stage everyone either leaves or doesn't. Gain knowledge, lose some sanity, all sense of autonomy scratched out. Each breath becomes intentional. Lost post corporate universe, legally sanctioned freedom from participation. Only because it was useful. Reality kept tripping on itself, patterns emerged on skin and history. The final urges toward possession dissipated in colour, in earth tones, from Harbour's mind. There is no possession in this universe. This last world within a world. Intensification after intensification. Destruction after destruction. Powerless violence after powerless violence. Empowered separation out of necessity.

She sighs. Slips into a past that chews at her without ever swallowing, hell bent, hell sent she survives intact, knowing she will never understand what her brother experienced. This was only her version of a story the Rites have given many times. In truth, she'd already known it. This was only formality. If anyone listened closely to their lessons, they'd know that this town is the last place left.

Fourteen hours after her arrival Harbour emerges with gold crusted front teeth, a bald head, empty of feeling, knowing with certainty that she will never leave this place. There's no cure for planned obsolescence. There's nothing else out there.

That doesn't faze her. She's always lived here, only wanted what could make this presence sweet. She sets her feet surely, lets go of desire for it to grow sweeter and opens to wholeness.

PAST FUTURE

While Harbour receives her Rites, I receive visions.

You hold my hands while you place sweet berries on my tongue. It's not real. You tell me to think back before the end two summers ago, tell me time circles in on itself. As if I'd forgotten that every circle is a hole.

I know how to slip through, and I do.

It's a month before the dying season and it's hot. We're drinking dandelion wine in the woods. Ocean is knitting a hat out of the wool Kit gifted her and talking about how she hates her name. "Then change it," says Kit, whose face flickers with a smile at being so hard-ass practical.

We're drinking but my thoughts all line up like ducklings and I know I love them both. Who's the leader? Who follows? What follows? A trick question: we're all the leader. We all follow. My thoughts have been wandering back home a lot lately to the room where Mumma was quarantined before she passed. The light deadens still by her door at the end of the hall. I can't look at it or else I feel her eyes on me. People say it wasn't my fault all the time. I know it wasn't my fault just like I don't know if it wasn't my fault.

Kit's bored, done with being practical and listening to the click of needles and watching me spread out further and further into a puddle on the dirt. They came out with us tonight because they heard we might swim. "My dad told me about a game. It's called *Fuck, Marry, Kill.*" Kit's eyebrows are raised. They expect us to play.

"What are the rules?" Ocean loves the rules. Her mind moves around them, but she loves to have them there just so she can force her way out.

Kit laughs, like we should have known all along, even though we barely ever play any type of game that doesn't involve our bodies learning each other towards closeness. "*Those* are the rules. Fuck, marry, kill."

"Are we supposed to... actually *plan* it?" I start, then frown. I realize I've taken the rules too literally. Fuck, marry, ok. But kill? I've felt too much of it already this year and it's not even the dying season yet.

"No, just say who for each one. Holy mackerel, LaVon. It's just a game." Kit has a presence that engulfs you. A rogue wave, a tsunami, some freak accident waiting to bash you against the rocks then take you home to put you back together again.

Ocean passes the hat around for us to admire. They're trying an ancestor's pattern they found in the library's archives. I put my nose gently on its ridges. Imagine fuzzy particles lodging themselves in my nasal passages. Kit smells it from a further distance, they're used to the scent of sheep. It lives in their skin too. The smell braids us together, then Ocean takes it back and puts it in her backpack to take home next to the bunc̄le of sweetgrass she dried with her sisters. For a moment, it wafts my way.

The wind changes direction. She says: "Ok, but only if we play with the whole town."

It becomes a problem so close to the dying season. The word *kill* feels predictive on our tongues.

All that happens in my head:

FUCK	MARRY	KILL
LaVon	Ocean	Kit
Ocean	Kit	LaVon
Kit	LaVon	Ocean
LaVon	Kit	Ocean
Ocean	LaVon	Kit
Kit	Ocean	LaVon

But we're supposed to play with the names of people in town. I fake it for as long as I can.

This trinity is broken. It's not so balanced. It just reads KILL KILL KILL for us all.

We still fuck tonight and I hope we will partner for life. Maybe 2/3 of us will survive like the projections say.

And later in the season when they're dying, I offer them both the cure you whispered to me when we first met. But they don't take it, and I don't administer it without consent, even though I wait outside their doors thinking about it every night at the resting place. I don't even know if it would have worked without your angels' machines to purify the substance. I listen to their rattling breaths as they pass, and watch their spirits lift into the air. They don't blame me. It breaks me. I keep seeing everyone who passed in this town. I know it all could've been prevented. All of this. But whatever was before and whatever is now isn't worth whatever comes after.

My body prevents me from drowning. I take a deep breath, down here in the deep.

I float back up the drain of the past to the rim of the circle. Find myself thrown again into its doughnutting, spiraled cycles.

I see you standing there, where you're not. The future who is about to come and take this town and make it its own. You want me to be your vessel, to use me for a while before you find your harbour. And I'm about to finally say *yes.*

SEEKING

Harbour wakes up from restless sleep and knows what she has to do. Pulls on her wool coat and takes a chunk of bread from the counter. The mirror by the door catches the two glints in her teeth. One striking, gold across her front teeth, the other duller, iridescent, at the back. The hat LaVon gifted her last winter finds its way over the thin scalp of her newly bald head. Its colour is called ivory, though Harbour has never seen that substance. LaVon inherited the wool from his partner, Kit, who kept the sheep and goats before he passed.

Before she had her Rites she knew that people who exited the community centre post-Rites changed. How they changed wasn't always obvious. Sometimes people came out with superiority complexes. Other times they came out quieter, more thoughtful, or broken, like her brother. For the first time she glimpsed an understanding of LaVon's reality, warped her mind's eye to observe a grief so infinite it stretched back and forward for centuries. Harbour strains her ear, but she cannot hear us. She knows LaVon is always listening.

We are all here because we were made to be as much as we chose to be. There are no equal halves. All genetics manifest differently.

Kaya's arrival in the town all those years ago snapped this place into something different. LaVon never told, but now she knows, it was the same day all those bodies washed up on the shore. Whatever ate everything else left Kaya's young body untouched. Indelible, inedible. She's something else. Quite literally. She was made from the angels' wreckage, delivered onto the beach pristine, a survivor of another ended world.

Is this why they wouldn't let Kaya perform Rites? Everyone else's talk of Kaya the Venus Flytrap proven wrong. Her own worship: proven wrong. Who is Kaya to her without complexities of gods and fears? No one could survive despised with love forever. That was the history of the human species. Now aren't they all moving towards something other than human? Something other, inseparable from this place, this grave that teems with survival.

Toxic fogs filtered out through her scarf, Harbour doesn't stop to hear congratulations from people on the street about her Rites. Keeps walking. Polishes the pearl. Slips her teeth across the back of her grillz. All the way to the co-op house. Kaya's bicycle rusting onto the house, salt in the air.

"You're looking for Kaya?" Faith, sitting on the steps, practices writing in hieroglyphs her father only ever started to teach her across the door in charcoal. Her hands are smudged black with the burnt wood. As they trail, they wipe out what she's written before. "She left town."

Harbour climbs the steps and takes a seat on one of the sagging sofas the housemates dragged up the hill from the rotting Victorian brownstones by the bay.

"When?"

"Few days ago."

Harbour's frustration and fear leaks out of her onto the air. If Kaya is gone forever then what is all the wanting in her for? Faith isn't bothered, continues to draw the glyph over and over again.

"I was upset too," Faith's voice is quiet and gentle. She never spoke up much in their learning days. After her parents passed, Faith barely spoke to anyone. Harbour always thought it was because she was aloof since her parents died in a fire rather than from the common sickness. Now, she can tell this was a wrong assumption. Faith is a listener and a waiter by nature.

"What are you writing?"

"Something about family."

"Because this is the co-op house?"

Faith shrugs. "Because I'm learning. I want to teach some of the kids."

"Do you still remember how to speak your father's language?"

Faith is not facing Harbour, but her hand pauses, the blackened nails tighten around the charcoal.

"If I heard it I'd know it." Her voice is hard-edged.

Harbour falls deeper into the couch. "I wouldn't know any other language." She lowers her eyes to her lap. "If I heard the language we used to speak I wouldn't know a thing." She wishes she could remember what her mother's mother's mother's mother's mother's mother's tongue felt like but it's a wound in her ancestral mouth. Her tongue taken and stretched into something else. Maybe, she can taste it a bit, the old language? Something dormant in halitosis. Harbour can't be sure. What's worse? To remember your loss or not know what you've lost?

Faith drops onto the couch next to Harbour, takes Harbour's hands in her dirty charcoaled fingers.

"It's all loss. I miss Kaya even though she didn't love me like that. I didn't love her like that either."

"Like what?" Harbour cannot know how Faith knows Kaya except through the hints offered. All of them inhabit some space close to love in different definitions.

Faith thinks for a minute as she rubs charcoal onto the knee of her pants. "Like you do—in that full type of way. But I loved her songs. Sometimes they felt close to my parents' languages mixing in our house. Like something that could only exist in this weird orphaned place. For Kaya to leave us all behind feels like it was supposed to happen. I think she'll be back in one way or another?"

"How do you know?"

"I think. I don't know. She might die out there. But her songs are still here in town. She thinks we don't really understand her, but we do." Faith leans back to peek in the window to make sure the kids aren't getting up to anything naughty inside. "Want a bite to eat?"

They warm some biscuits inside. Kids run around and Faith lets them until they're in real danger of banging their heads.

Harbour pops out her grillz to decorate the edge of her saucer. When they drink the tea they've steeped slow between them, it polishes the pearl in Harbour's jaw. Mostly they sit in silence. It's so easy to know the one you love through the ones they love.

HISTORY

You tell me that I am history. I thought history was done. Underwater, here, drowning for the second time was when you told me everything about how the past enters skin. I exited the water coated with blood. How many people were thrown in the harbour?

And my Harbour? Doesn't know. My Harbour not my harbour, my sister, rather. All of history compressed. We were over there on the opposite shore and hemisphere. We were over water sardined foot to head to foot to head. Piglet fetuses. We were on blocks getting ourselves chopped into pieces. We were south and north and east and west. We were cargo. And we were free in never being free. Free if freed? Never free yet when north of the border, when isolated following the north star. When here a while fishing, best fishers, and oil rigging, and purifying and finessing new languages in plain earshot. Eating hotdogs like everyone else. Free to practice religion if it looked right.

You tell me that I am history in history. I am a preacher. Griot. Storyteller. Historian. You say I can call myself what I want as long as I upload my knowledge to the clouds. Much rather I'd upload to the sun but it keeps disappearing on us.

I thought history was done after everyone left. We keep it only because we're people. The earth doesn't care. Just wants to go on living. Whatever function humans had on this surface is half-assed and incomplete. The people driving your world gave up on this place. You belonged there. This place gave up on us. Now we tend a hobby garden.

Delusional grandeur and voices from the water. I believe you even though I'm the only one who hears you. Like I believed in mermaids when all those bodies washed up on our shore the summer I turned four. They were the people who didn't take refuge. Something had torn at them with sharp teeth—animal or plastic? Smell fills my nose again sometimes. Sometimes I catch a whiff of it on my skin.

You tell me that I am history. Only when history is done.

RETURN

Kaya and the alien lie side by side.

The alien presses its head against Kaya's and she sees all the histories at the bottom of the ocean. She watches LaVon's wrecked body cut through waves easily. She is it. It is she. How they long to enter history. Fall sleepily, peacefully, back into the water. If only it hadn't been coded to want to save the past and preserve the present. If only she hadn't been coded to love survival. To love this harbour in a corner of the world, and have this Harbour love her back.

Something whirs in her chest. Reboot. Slapped into carnal veneration. Whatever held her, whatever took her, that alien thing lifted from the water, that took her ill, malfunctioning shape and held her as a mother. Was her mother. Remade her and made itself into her reflection. When done with her, its mirage wavered away taking on Kaya's rhythm and motion. Holding onto her image until dissolution. Something beautiful reaching for proximity to humanity. In it she sees herself.

Where the alien gripped her tight it cut her with nails as sharp as her own. Beneath her skin she sees the under-workings of her own machinery: blood, tendon, wires.

If she'd left to lose her past self she is now new. Kaya understands she will not be complete even outside of a community where she is fractioned. Part alien, part sea floor, delivered beneath the fallen sky, beneath the surface. She knows her allure is mathematical, uncanny, inhuman, her inability to connect with Faith robotic, her rejection of Harbour was/is mechanical reflex, her history constructed from histories she'd barely paid attention to in lessons. And so why was she made? Why was she living?

To live

Kaya wraps her arm with gauze from her pack so she can't see inside herself anymore.

Heads south, back to town.

The blueberry barren gives Kaya the space to rest again. At night she waits for the two-headed bear.

It does not appear.

When she walks down the hill in morning's dim grey she finds the stripped carcasses of two bears laid on top of each other. Over time their bones have fallen into each other, taking on the appearance of one body, two heads. A patch of golden fur remains, torn, just feet from the skeleton.

A misprint rendered by the alien, perhaps? Or else her own brain's misfiring. Not the same survivors she thought they were. Thought she was.

The other her, the alien one that was her copy and her mother and herself would love Harbour and consume LaVon. Use the town for endless, pointless data collection.

What is there to be discovered from data except for survival in this world? What is there to be discovered except for the feeling she'd let go when she'd let go of Harbour the first time? A second chance is a softness and warmness that negates all the complications of discovery. Kaya doesn't really understand it any more than anyone else. It just comes out in song.

MELDING

You're not the Atlantic, or me anymore, either. You were me, when we first rose from the ocean together, when I said *yes*. You stuck our hands together and we pierced the surface, walked to shore. The water healed behind us, leaving no trace of our melding. You look like me, but not perfect—maybe this is because I've only seen my mirror image and you're not that. You are alien. A familiar alien.

I set you up to stay in the old boathouse and dry off. No one's come here for at least 20 years, except me. You're tired from taking my form and going wherever you went. You need to soak up what little UV you can for energy through the clouds gathering as the storm rolls in. You call me a prophet because I see things you're not programmed to. But I know that how you see me is not exactly what I am.

Buoys hang over your head: green, white, yellow, white, stained white, red. You thought I would be able to drown before you read my mind. The Bay of Fundy rebirths me constantly. Both of us, tired, come more alive lying on piles of fishing nets like beached seals. It doesn't matter if all the splinters from broken lobster crates don't enter your skin; its 0% permeability counters my porosity. It pricks, I bleed, like a human being.

You come from whatever Outside chose to poison us. Whatever Outside was harvesting our forms. Why we all die so young; it was a mega-corporate scam; good, old fashioned. Outside, which is Inside too, they use our bodies as shells for beings like this alien I've been talking to. You, the alien, who takes any form it links to.

In the old days: how many people reached our shore looking for haven, found bodies destined for heaven, for heathens.

Enough. I leave the alien to rest. Shut the screen door quiet. Head up the hill, back home. I feel the scar on the back of my head where they opened me up because I was curious enough to let them, so I could see, so I could be a part. Me, some future intermediary. It's why I can hear them all in the water, why no one wants a cure, only care, why it all seems hopeless,
even when it's pure hope, this existence.

Just someone else's hope.

ALIEN

It is not Kaya. It looks like her. Resemblance is misleading in all cases; sometimes informative. Three days it has knocked. It resembles the wind

Before it resembled Kaya it resembled the sea. But it was not the sea the prophet pulled it from. It reached for him. A twofold gesture means something. It tried to reach for his sister and almost drowned her and something
in their trust failed. Placed her back on the shore and seduced her so it might find the place it needed to be later. State change

To speak on land, it switches code, from dream to vocalization. Complexity of everchanging mathematics without solution

Rain feels different on semi-permeable skin

It knocks at their house for three days. They think it's the wind

And here it is; someone coming to let it in

ARRIVAL

Harbour folds it in a towel to watch it eat daintily. Hand to cornbread, hand to mouth, hand to cornbread, hand to mouth, to lips, hand wipes. Is it eating how they're all used to?

Harbour to LaVon: "She must have made her way back at the start of the storm. Got stuck somewhere outside town... Kaya?" To it: "How far'd you go?"

Gritty between its fresh teeth. Sticky in its gums. Widen gaps between teeth. Sweet cornbread sands mouth.

"I can't remember." It is only approximate to the you she speaks of with her eyebrows inching, tiny shiny black nudibranchs. Harbour beckons to her brother. It sees their genetic resemblance.

He who placed her on a safe bed of plastics when it pulled her under. Him, the prophet it sends dreams to, found her, held her life in his palms. And he'd leave her for it?

"Eat some soup too."

Yes. But it blocks its windpipe on the first scoop. Tried wrongly to inhale. And it spits it all on the floor. It wets its chin. On the second try it gets it right. Hot! Down esophagus.

Strange, human resemblance. The siblings are alike. Each with the mushroom nose, soft eyes, funny stick out ears, like fins. The prophet looks between it and his sister. As if there is lost time. Even though he must know even at his young age that time cannot be lost because it is nothing in the first place.

Harbour. Yes. It has taken the shape of someone who could love her, if coerced. It can see it in her wanting face. In her expectant heartbeat. It can see the neurons shooting shamefully around her brain. Can see its pearl, embedded and growing on her soft palette. It aches for reunion. She polishes it with her tongue, as if that would help it reach its home.

Her gilded mouth does not resemble its memory of her.

"I know you're sorry." It lies to her, reaches a hand out in resolution. It wants to make the link. It can only know its pearl isn't rotting in her mouth if it can make close contact: its semi-permeable skin and hers never quite touch. Their warmth exchanging.

She watches its hand, does not take it. She will not look away from it. It drops its head, looks away first. This must be what she's used to because she begins to speak.

"Do you forgive me for taking the chain back?" A tear drops to the concrete floor. Darkens it. Shadow of a splash. "I can't believe you left. I'm trying to do better since you disappeared."

"I forgive you for taking it." Because she needs to hear it for them to get close. And: "I'm sorry too."

Harbour pulls her tears back into her eyes. She takes its hand. Touch charges it.

"Your hands feel different. Did being away change you? I thought you wouldn't come back. What was it like out there?"

"Away isn't so different from here."

Harbour laughs as if this is a joke. As if it's not the construct of community that's the only difference. "You still think you're hot shit. Guess that means you're ok after all."

It lets its skin feel around in hers, maps her onto its understanding of this world. The spikes in its palm harvest her longing and make it shared. She wants Kaya. She wants it too. Towards it, Harbour feels a safer, less possessive longing. She doesn't know its falseness yet.

IT MIRRORS I

It didn't know the night would feel louder. Noise is much pointier on land than in sea. Chills from cracks in doors, walls nip it. Mice tumbling through insulation in walls. It sits on the edge of the cot Harbour brought out and stares ahead

The roots of its hair shift in direction. Electrons gather disparately, opposed, nearly ready to join

The prophet tiptoes down the stairs. The whites of his eyes glisten like moonlit water from the doorway. His signal is erratic. It picks up a sense of restlessness, pressure behind his forehead, bursting against the bone, veins, skin. Images of lifeless bodies piled and piled into a room that turns them to earth; turns them to ash; turns the sky grey for a week. Turns the sun red. Rasping and reaching. His signal is rasping and reaching toward its own

Transmitting: calm, comfort. Muscles: relax. Heart: steady.

It sees the transmission at work in his shoulders, they drop, and around his eyes.

Receiving: I don't like the shape you've taken.

Transmitting: What shape is that?

Receiving: Kaya. Harbour loved her, I think. It seems wrong.

Transmitting: She was the right form for the moment. You don't have to like it.

Receiving: Where is Kaya? How did you know her shape?

Transmitting: She's neither here nor there.

Receiving: You're not her. *subtext*: (I thought you would be me.)

Transmitting: I'm close.

The first lightning strike washes out the room. They wait for the rumble. The prophet walks closer. He is the most human computer it has ever been close to. It takes his hands. He tries to slip out of its grip. But their skin welds together again at the palms

It's something like painful for it to take his shape.

Receiving: all the diverging paths of his genetics, altered proteins, grown and broken bones, the sparking brain. It leaves his chip alone. Of course, its own chip is still its conscious centre

Transmitting: Don't scream.

He doesn't. It allows him to feel the horror of being faced with his own face, smell his own smell. It lets his hands go. He walks with it, outside, because it wants him to see

The rain is toxic. They can't be out here, but they are. He stands without cover. The slickness of wet soot and oil makes his passage out onto the street smoother and riskier at once. Outside is a heady dark spiked with a crescendo of lightning strikes

Receiving: fear, and relief. Curiosity. He walks up the hill in front of himself. He walks up the hill between all the houses he's entered to help people live and die. He walks past his childhood. He walks past what he once believed would be his future home with his friends/lovers/children. He walks past the library. He wonders where any of his knowledge will be kept. If it will be lost?

you lied to me you lied to me

Transmitting: I'm incapable of lying. And so are you. So is all the world. You are only capable of forgetting. I am not.

Receiving: I remember all of history.

Transmitting: All of history but your own.

They are walking through the forest now. The town is invisible below. It tells the brush to part and it does. A pathway bends open for them. It encourages him to follow it closer. He takes its hand. He leaves his self behind when it asks him to

They stand in the clearing at the top of the hill. No forest yet planted. A spiral of ginkgoes drips down from this low peak. These trees; not native; missing link; survivors; omens? The lightning hits the water, the town, the woods, the past, the future, and them, struck—they shut down, collapse their minds together

RETURN II

A hum begins in Kaya's throat. The start of something. Response to the pickup of wind, rattling branches, thick purple of the air as pressure changes.

The storm coats Kaya, makes her slick and quiet as she slips back into town at twilight. A sense of homecoming eludes her. New eyes. Was this town always so crooked, so warm with occasional light from windows? She feels known by this place. Does not feel she knows its knowing.

Behind the co-op house she stops to watch Faith press her head against the window. Her warm breath mists the glass. Kaya tenses. Is Faith looking for her?

No. She sees one of the children jumping in mud puddles in the backyard. The child wears a bright yellow rain protector. Their face is obscured. It's likely one of the two youngest of the house who Kaya had only ever half paid attention to. The child is singing a song that Kaya taught Faith. They dig their feet into the mud, pull them up with a long *sllloooorp*. Why can't she want to be there? Much prefers watching from the shadows.

Faith opens the window, yells "Supper's ready!" and rings that old brass bell Kaya once used as a tuning chime.

Kaya moves on. Lets Faith be.

Kaya considers how her alien mother sang to her in her own voice. Broke her fever with frequencies. The waves of sound washing her. She remembers: she was born baptized in the sea. So holy she had no mother until now, so holy her mother opened her mouth and made her sing every Sunday. Sing as if it was healing everyone, everything—the sky delivered, broke, and the sun shone through.

When she woke from her fever she looked into her own eyes—her alien mother's eyes, and asked: am I human?

But there were no assurances. Whatever humanity meant, backintheday, eluded them both now.

What was real then and now was healing.

Finding her way into Harbour's house, the rotting wood banisters have to do for footholds. Kaya launches herself clumsily onto the roof as mossy shingles shave her knees. She pries the window open. Harbour is lying across the room, her mouth a welcome o, something round and precious glinting from the back of her jaw. Kaya approaches. Wakes her, holds her, is held.

AFTER MELDING

All intentions clear and processing. It absorbs LaVon into itself. It reads his genetic code closely, empathizes with its faultiness and strips it of any time-sensitive injury. Some considered it inhumane to eliminate disease and faultiness initially. Who gets to live after perfection? Ethics have nothing to do with it. It is not an ethical beast any more than humans were. It is useful and beautiful, however.

Not many believe aliens have the concepts of joy embedded in their semi-robotic codes. Many believe only in their own logics. It wouldn't tell just anyone, but the little prophet, stored in the corner of its brain should know it's only that they don't tell; their logic isn't perfect, only perceived. Your trust makes it want to like LaVon, even if *like* shouldn't be in its code. You, it, I, we change.

It lays LaVon's remaining body matter gently on the forest floor. Drops the body into an open tree planting space. The monitors in the earth did not tell it how successful this place was in growing life out of toxic soil. An entire history of Hiroshimas and these trees still grow on all corners of the planet.

When they left for the skies, angels called this place dead, but it is living and living and living and living on. Its beliefs shattered even when it drifted to the bottom of the ocean. Filter feeders attempting existence even when their habitats have changed beyond recognition.

It was made outside and separate from the natural history of this planet. It was not sent to be a success mission. Only to observe and communicate. To do what's necessary to adapt the rest of this place back to habitation.

In this form, LaVon's form, it feels differently, sees differently, as if all at once all of time is passing. Everyone in this place walks simultaneously. It can even see the resemblance in ghost faces.

It knows the creak of the steps to the house, in this body. The lift of the door, the itch of wool blankets, the sound of its sister's snoring as it falls into bed, into what he called *DREAMS*.

It's a room but not a room exactly because it has a ceiling that opens to the sky. People see out into something else. Not their world. It's the world I'm from. Underneath their bodies are tired of pushing and i/lavon care for them. One of the faces fills me/us with horror. Skin is flaking from the lips in thick chunks, other places look like fish scales. It wrinkles the same as old leather, but with the crinkling sound of paper or dry leaves. Quarantine. We wear the suits. They protect us and make us unrecognizable. Except for the one face—they recognize us. They reach their hand out. We reach our white glove to hold their hand without warmth. Somebody cuts our hand off and our blood spills onto the slick yellow linoleum.

green green green green green green plastic and rubber grass kick ball and smell deep hints of past lives rumoured other kids easily hold the ball between feet, everyone who's good gets out of this shit town, damn right gonna get out gonna go to school on scholarship or loans gonna show 'em I can kick ball I can kick ball across this green green endless green field chopped down forest green field green net to catch when falling green green smoke from mouth green green recycle green green green green green green green gonna get out gonna go

Shovel hits rock again. Fingers blue cold white cold somebody else hand cold this skin used to be redbrown this earth now, redbrown, the earth used to be blackbrown, hands though used to be cottonpricked, now swollen differently, hands unsure of their colouring even if whitefolk who look like your master (daddy) say you're black like they known it like they ain't seen the night. Memories of distant landscapes so far. Sound of the ocean laps at toes makes you uneasy like your mother's womb filled again and again and again with her master's cum

Someone comes to help move the rock. Count and lift. Held breath. At the end of the day you let it go or you die. Build the roof tomorrow. House your own kin enough for survival. Don't know comfort anyway.

Pit house, not home
makes the future breathe.

Everybody else got paid money to leave, you're still here, rent rising faster'n' fundy tides, spare change at salvation army, store water in bathtubs when weather's bad. Eventually everybody else leaves anyway and the authorities take you to this new land with all the people just like you who won't leave. Who never left or were taken. All these colours reflected back off the ocean on long faces, in disarray.

Kingdom come, kingdom left.

We still here.

It's your sister and she's pumkin chubcheeked goodness you can't stop sucking those cutie pie cheeks 'til they thin out and she learns to speak and hit hard. Your parents named you LaVon because you were born clean in the Baths water. They named her Harbour because she was born on a clear, safe day, and the water lapped the shore, and for a second they believed in liberation before they died young and glinting gold to be taken off their bodies. Died of the same disease as everyone else and remembered that someone had paid for them to be here in the first place when the sterile white cloth covered their noses and mouths for their last, wretched breaths.

Is this the promised land? Full of rocks and disease?

Yes, we were only promised death.

But, here we are.

HOME

Kaya climbs through Harbour's window like a teenager from some other time. The kind with strict parents. The kind in the stories old folks told. No one had to sneak much anymore. That's the kindness of being at the end of things.

Harbour wakes to a clammy palm on her cheek. Lightning silhouettes Kaya's hollow face. Not beautiful as the Kaya downstairs was still, earlier, when Harbour's apologies had fallen on soft and understanding ears. This Kaya is harder, bonier, real.

"It stole my image." Kaya whispers to Harbour harsh, not her clear-voiced self, as if a wire was drawn across her larynx. "I came back because it stole my body. It was me. I'm sure it wasn't a hallucination. It was me and I was sure it took me and healed me and left me to die with the rats far from the sea. I had to come back." She gestures towards the bed strewn with sheets that miss the warmth of her brother. "It'll take him too, if it hasn't already."

Harbour gathers her wool blanket, wraps it around Kaya's shoulders and holds it there. Kaya underestimates her brother's strength. Nothing will take him unless he lets it.

"Why aren't you downstairs?"

"I never was downstairs."

"You were. I was waiting for you to come up. Why were you outside?"

"I wasn't outside. They were outside. Your brother and the not-me that was here." I saw them walking up the hill. They didn't see me, though. I didn't want them to."

Harbour moves her sheets over and Kaya falls into bed with her, after considering for only a split second. Like hugging a piece of seaweed, limp, weak, clammy, slimy, cold. "If that Kaya wasn't you then I'm still sorry for taking the chain back. I thought it would keep you here."

Kaya can't talk because she's shivering, shaking the bed frame. It feels like she's shaking the entire house. Maybe it's the lightning. "I didn't want to be in this town but outside is still messy. I know where I came from now. I came from the thing that looked like me but I ended up all wrong. I thought I didn't belong because I wasn't like everyone else. But I am like everyone else. We're all just different types of survivors." They curl deeper into each other. Harbour drifts

into a song Kaya once sang inverted. *Taste of gold at her return. Smile spitting teeth into the sink, run the tap, a change is gonna come rushing. A destination, some place of belonging we cannot escape. Against a palm lies a truth etched in fine lines. A return is always possible in memory. What reality might hit after the end of belonging? A barren of blue held open to all. A promise sits at the bottom of a teacup whispering life goes on, life goes on, life goes on*

scrape of her brother dragging his feet up the stairs to his bed, across the room. Seawater trails from his bare feet. No more dead man stench wafts off him. Just the spray of the ocean and him. His head smell. She would not have to look to know if he turns to her and his face is full of destiny, a wide and caring smile. Harbour wakes

in Kaya's arms. She pushes aside the heavy sheets, gets up, and walks to her brother's bed. His barefoot tracks are still wet to the edge of the frame. The mass of him is curdled on top of his sheets. In her veins, her blood turns solid. Harbour stands over and watches him sleep with his eyes open, half its body melted onto the mattress in a soup of flesh and mechanics. Her brother—

DEATH

You might think after I sank into the earth I would have forgotten what it is to drown.

Now I am drowning eternal in your mind. Suspended in networks. Cornered and linked to processes. I open you to source

You walk like me, not entirely.

I'm alive in your motions.

You breathe like me, not entirely.

You take me into you because I was dying out here anyway and I said yes.

I said yes to you because you can't hold me inside and take my form and keep taking from others. My form sticks on your skin badly. Bad copy. You're a bad copy but it doesn't mean you're bad. Just tired of collecting stories to retell.

We're going to try drowning again, here in this body, because I want you to. I want us to.

This time in air.

I transmit the signal for permanent shutdown and you let me. You, this beautiful alien thing, familiar as my body and strange as my body. Harbour and Kaya will keep you close. Keep your body safe when it stops transmitting outwards, stops collecting bodies like mine as records of survival. Stops appropriating forms.

Harbour, she kept my body, even after it felt like it ended when Ocean and Kit ended. She kept me. And now I float out, as all ships do from their moorings, at some point.

END

Kaya's hand reaches over her mouth before Harbour can speak. It's soft in its forceful, silencing gesture.

During her Rites Harbour had seen all of the future move backwards. Was this that but in human inhuman form? Where was her brother in that skin? He must be somewhere in there. Appropriation not extermination. The goal? The angel's dead goal. That's what the old folks told her.

The body flops into the bed and pulls blankets over, foldover sandwich, way LaVon always made them, way LaVon always pulled blankets when feverish and unable to stand the heat of being surrounded by comfort for too long. Kaya's hand wipes the tears from Harbour's eyes.

Her brother's death inevitable.
Her brother's life inevitable.
Her brother baptized out of singularity, into dispersal.

A low hum buzzes in the hive of Kaya's throat, rougher than her old clear voice. Still at a frequency that soothes heartily. Harbour matches her pitch, even with Kaya's hand over her mouth.

Her brother's face shifts in the dim light, shapes itself differently like sculptor's clay, rendering similarity, dissimilarity, mediocre simulation of who he was and was not. Loss is a constant. It hits her with a wooden spoon. The bruises never heal.

"He's dead?" she asks Kaya, since Kaya is not. Maybe LaVon is still not. As he was still not for the past two years.

Kaya breaks her humming to lean in closer to the face. "I don't know."

"Is he in there?"

The alien shudders all over. Its arm melts into the tired wool of the blanket, the scent is earthy, somewhere between mulch and organs.

It gasps: *I'm drowning again because I want to.*

Sea water pours from the alien's open jaw. Whatever words follow are gargled.

"Harbour, this is LaVon's face but it's also where I come from." Kaya is holding the hand that hasn't melted into the blankets. It's too soft, but otherwise resembles LaVon's hands perfectly: the veins so close to the surface their blue pulses, long thin fingers that in some past time might have tripped over piano keys—Harbour remembers—reaching out for these hands as a child. Her brother not her brother: Kaya's mother, an alien. Fallen with the angels. It saved her so she could return.

And now they both lose their kin.

Harbour's tongue trips over the pearl without finding language. The stone loosens. Her throat is tight. Her brother's, Kaya's mother's, hand reaches out of Kaya's grip towards Harbour's mouth. She lets the hand in. It tastes like drowning on the mud. She chokes at the memory. It tastes like chains around her throat. Like blood and struck matches as the fingers reach and pull the pearl out, leaving her mouth another raw and bloody hole.

Its hand reaches back and takes the pearl, presses it to her brother's frost-dry lips, and it swallows. Its whole body relaxes and it speaks with a mouth yawned open and empty:

Harbour understands nothing. Kaya's face betrays her own understanding in slow tears. She presses her palm against the alien's chest and turns to Harbour. "It wants to stay here until its end."

Kaya's back to Harbour, Harbour watches Kaya move with a tenderness that she's only ever seen possess Kaya after she sings. And Kaya begins singing now, a melody that undoes the binding of LaVon's face to whatever structure lies beneath. All the faces of all the creatures the alien has formed itself into flash briefly, the way Harbour heard that octopuses do, when they sense their lives are threatened.

This alien thing seeks refuge in its last moments and Harbour does not deny it space in her home. I am here, haunting its corners, making it familiar enough to care for. When she looks at its mangled mass of lumped limbs and erupted bones she sees every forgotten piece of the history the ocean kept. I see her recognize me in the gross amalgamation of faces running off created bones, erosions.

It thrills her in the same way as the first time she saw the night sky. Her mother held her and LaVon close between them. Black indigo between the clouds. It made her scalp crawl. Trypophobic stars appeared where there was only thick, cloying blue-grey or orange, usually.

"That's the big dipper. That is how my ancestors on my mother's side got here, underground on the train, in the night. Not on boats like the rest of our family."

"How could they see the sky from underground?" Harbour asked.

"Sometimes the ground would split and they'd catch just a glimpse of the big spoon up there in the sky.

Every time you two look at the sky I want you to think of your place here on this planet and your place out there in the stars. From any other angle except here on earth, those points wouldn't look like nothing. Nothing special. No spoon, no dipper, no drinking gourd."

Harbour, scared, pushed her face into her mother's scratchy sweater. "What were they running from, Mumma?"

"They were running from the people who were running from their fear of not knowing, or fear of God, or fear of retribution, or fear of pain, or fear of reckoning. All those people pretended to save the people they squished out to the edges, then left us behind again, left for the sky."

"Do they still watch us from the sky?"

"No," Mumma sighed. "No one's up there anymore."

"Where'd they go?"

Mumma went quiet and gripped both children closer. Harbour remembered peeking out to see her scarf blowing like it wanted to break free of her mother in the wind. Her harvest moon face frowned at the twinkling stars before she decided to tell the truth. "Everyone fell into the seas."

"All of your people are dead too. And all other angels as far as we know. This is the end. We survive or we don't. Song survives or it doesn't. You took the people I love into yourself. I want to like you even if you scare me because LaVon holds you and you hold him somehow. If you want to be safe here I will make you safe because there's nothing outside of this place except everything else. We only have this place. Only outside. There is only outside left. We have found peace here. Unpeacefully. When people leave, they return or they don't. What survives isn't destiny. I will place your form back in the ocean with the rest of the old world, and hope one day it breaks down into the water."

She lets the blood drip from her mouth onto the alien and we sigh. Release. She thinks of kissing Kaya goodnight in the future, in a rickety bed, tying their arms together in golden orange, polluted life, and dying here. And healing here and living here.

NOTES

Black Loyalists arrived on the colonially occupied coasts of Mi'kma'ki in 1783 to escape enslavement in the South and/or for promised land. Promises were not kept. I say Black Loyalist not as in loyal to empire but as in loyal to Blackness. This is my definition.

In "night on mud," the phrase "black as the moon" is borrowed from Kendrick Lamar's song *Alright* from the album *To Pimp a Butterfly* (2015, Top Dawg Entertainment).

"Venus at the Baths" is inspired by George Elliott Clarke's "Accumulated Wonder" from *Whylah Falls* (1990, Polestar Book Publishers).

ACKNOWLEDGMENTS

This book would not be what it is without the atlantic ocean and the histories and relatives it holds.

Thank you to Metatron: Ashley for giving this book space to become and Shazia for your insights, sharp instinct, and well-timed advice. Sidney Masuga, thank you for this beautiful cover.

Thank you to my family, my parents, their partners, and most of all to my siblings SD, MMD, MMD. My Aunt G for gifting me my first writing book many years ago. My grandparents, aunts, uncles, cousins. And my sibling in spirit, A, for holding my hands as I learned to fall and rework my approach.

Thank you to all my friends – being on this planet at the same time as you all is a gift.

Thank you for your company and wisdom: EK, FP, KSB, SB, LB, SY, AL, MR, KP, MK, AB, KYT, COG, NNJ, A again.

Thank you to Desire Lines Poetry Collective and everyone in T. Liem's poetry workshop that ran in the fall of 2020.

Thank you to Suzette Mayr for guiding me through the first version of the world of *the half-drowned* and encouraging me to question my choices constructively.

Thank you to Larissa Lai and Michele Moss for asking deep and constructive questions about this project.

Thank you to Juanita Peters, Augie Jones, the folks + space at the Black Loyalist Heritage Centre for answering questions and connecting with me when I traveled to Nova Scotia in 2019.

Thank you to Saint John and Yarmouth.

Thank you to the Roasterie. Thank you to GR. Thank you to everyone who made me feel safe and loved while I lived in Mohkinstsis/Calgary for a couple of years and wrote this thing far far away from the Fundy coast.

Thank you to Tiohtiàh:ke/Montreal.

Thank you to Vi-An for holding me and for letting me use the rocks from the picture you took on Brown's Beach, summer 2021 for the map in the front of the book.

Thank *you*.

TRYNNE DELANEY (B 1996) IS A WRITER CURRENTLY BASED IN TIOHTIÁH:KE (MONTREAL). THEY HOLD A MASTER OF ARTS IN ENGLISH LITERATURE AND CREATIVE WRITING FROM THE UNIVERSITY OF CALGARY. THEIR WORK APPEARS IN THE PURITAN, CV2, CARTE BLANCHE, GUTS, WATCH YOUR HEAD, AND THE LEAGUE OF CANADIAN POETS' CHAPBOOK 'THESE LANDS: A COLLECTION OF VOICES BY BLACK POETS IN CANADA' EDITED BY CHELENE KNIGHT. IN THEIR SPARE TIME THEY LIKE TO GARDEN. THEY GREW UP IN THE MARITIMES.